Eerie McLeery

Jan Burchett and Sara Vogler were already friends when they discovered that they both wanted to write books for children – and that it was much more fun to write together. They meet every weekday for gossip, jokes and writing. If one is stuck for an idea, the other always comes up with something, or makes a cup of tea. They both have two children who are always their first audience.

Jan used to be a primary school teacher and lives in Essex. Sara used to be a midwife and lives in London.

All Little Terrors titles can be ordered at your local bookshop or
are available by post from Bookpost (tel: 01624 836000).

Little Terrors

EERIE McLEERY

Jan Burchett and Sara Vogler

Illustrated by Judy Brown

MACMILLAN
CHILDREN'S BOOKS

For Tony Bradman who gave us a lot of help
and still thinks we're one person

First published 1998 by Macmillan Children's Books
This edition produced 2002 for
The Book People Ltd, Hall Wood Avenue,
Haydock, St Helens WA11 9UL

ISBN 0 330 36813 3

7 9 8 6

A CIP catalogue record for this book is available from the British Library.

Typeset by SX Composing DTP, Rayleigh, Essex
Printed and bound in Great Britain by Mackays of Chatham plc, Kent

Chapter One

A piercing shriek shattered the air at Little Frightley Manor. It resounded in the cavernous basement and rang round the medieval battlements, sending hordes of pigeons into the air in fright. It echoed through the ancient hall, up the stone stairs, across the shadowy gallery, and hit George Brussell's ears as he lay snoring in his bedroom in the Victorian tower. George sat bolt upright in his four-poster bed, his hair standing on end.

"Georgie! You'll be late for school."

George glared at his school uniform which gloated at him from a chair. He couldn't believe the summer holidays were over.

George's mother's shriek was enough to waken the dead – and it did. It woke every one of the ghosts of Little Frightley Manor.

1

For most ghosts the night is the busiest time, but these particular spirits needed to recharge their spectral batteries and couldn't do without their sleep. Not that they had any intention of doing normal ghostly things like wailing and chain-rattling and leaving bloodstains all over the house. After all, they didn't have any blood, and anyway, that sort of behaviour was for grown-up ghouls.

The seven little ghosts belonged to the noble Ghoulstone family who had built and lived in Little Frightley Manor for over seven hundred years. After the sad death of Lady Cecily, the last living Ghoulstone, when the portrait of an ancestor fell on her head, the Brussells had moved in, and although the ghosts were great friends with George, they had no intention of sharing the house with his parents. Sharren and Darren Brussell wouldn't see a ghost if it bit them, but Darren was larger than life, and Sharren could outshriek any spectre. So the seven ghosts lived in a luxury caravan in the grounds at the front of the massive old house.

Maggot Ghoulstone, shimmering gently in his sleep, was rudely awakened by Sharren's shriek and fell out of the top bunk, hitting the thick pile carpet with a spectral plop. Maggot was a sooty ghost, wearing a scorched sailor suit. His snub nose was red from a cold he caught the day before he died, and was now stuck with.

"Spooktacular landing, Maggot!" sneered his twin sister, Flo, as she jumped out of bed and stepped over him.

Flo straightened her burnt, tattered petticoats and checked her frizzled ringlets in the gold-framed mirror. Her bright blue eyes stared back from her mucky, mischievous face. She did this every morning, although her appearance hadn't changed since 1857, when she and Maggot had been blown up. They'd been tinkering with the engine of their father's latest invention – the horseless cart. In the spirit of scientific inquiry, they had added bananas to the fuel to make the cart go with a bang. And it did. It blew up the cart, the laboratory, the old west wing of Little Frightley Manor, and the eight-year-old twins. Maggot still smelt of bananas.

"Shake a leg, you lubbers," growled a gruff voice from the other end of the caravan.

Mary Ghoulstone, once the most feared nine-year-old pirate on the high seas, swung out of her hammock and scrambled up through the skylight to check for marauders. She was always hoping that, one morning, a proper marauder would

4

turn up, but the only invaders she ever saw were the milkman and the postman, and they never attacked the caravan, much to her disappointment. She stood astride the roof, a fearsome sight with her dark, heavy eyebrows, wild brown hair, tattered trousers, and dagger sticking out of her chest.

Duck, her one-eyed green parrot, flew up to her shoulder. "George to starboard!" he shrieked, adjusting his eyepatch. He'd lost his eye in an argument with a swordfish and he thought the patch, with its skull-and-crossbones design, made him look extremely fierce.

Mary and Duck watched as George slammed the front door of Little Frightley Manor and slouched miserably across the courtyard to wait for his mother by the portcullis. He clutched his bulging school bag in one hand and was cramming a piece of toast into his freckly face with the other. He'd had a fight with his school uniform, his shoelaces were in knots and his spiky

brown hair hadn't seen a comb for some time. It was a lovely sunny day, but even the ghastly gargoyles on the battlements were looking more cheerful than George.

Mary jumped down into the caravan just as Maggot was struggling to his feet. She sent him sprawling under the table.

"There be trouble a-brewing!" she yelled, pointing with her cutlass towards the house and nearly cutting Maggot's nose off as he tried to get up.

Flo ran to the window. Maggot followed, rubbing his spectral bruises and muttering curses at Mary – in a very low voice. He'd learnt the hard way not to argue with a pirate, especially a pirate who had been the scourge of the Spanish Main.

"Oh, no!" gasped Flo, looking towards the house. "George can't be going back to school already!"

When you've been dead for years and never have any birthdays, you don't notice time passing like the living do.

"But I wanted to play Get the Ghoul

today!" wailed Maggot, sniffing and wiping his nose on his sooty sleeve.

"I don't know why he's bothering with school," said Mary grumpily. "I never went and it never did me no harm."

"Didn't do you much good either," said Flo, pointing at the dagger that Captain Redbeard, Mary's mortal enemy, had stuck in her chest when she wasn't looking.

"Blood and guts!" squawked Duck.

Duck had died in the same sea battle as Mary, when Redbeard's cabin boy had tied

his wings behind his back and forced him to walk the plank.

The little ghosts loved messing about with George. George was a straightforward and most unusual boy who took ghosts in his stride, and, since he'd arrived, they'd come to life – as far as spooks *can* come to life. But at the thought of George going to school, their shimmer lost some of its shine and they felt their spectral stuffing sag with disappointment. It was like being a sparkler on its last splutter at a fireworks party.

A piece of ghostly paper fluttered sadly out from the bedroom. Maggot reached for it, but Flo snatched it out of his hand and read it aloud.

School
by Bartholomew Otherington-Smythe

1. I did not go to school.
2. I had no uniform.
3. I was a poor relation of the Ghoulstones, and lived in the attic of Little Frightley Manor.
4. My mother was my only teacher.

5. *I would love to attend George's school.*
6. *But I still have no uniform.*
7. *I would probably be too scared anyway.*
8. *Oh dear!*

Bartholomew Otherington-Smythe, Boss to his friends, was a timid thirteen-year-old spook who spent his time quivering invisibly and writing lists on ghostly paper. He never spoke and he couldn't be seen, even by the other ghosts, who only knew where he was when one of his lists appeared.

Flo's eyes suddenly lit up.

"Brilliant idea, Boss!" she yelled.

"What?" scoffed Maggot. "Being scared?"

"No, you turnip!" shouted Flo, hitting him over the head with the list. "Let's all go to school – with George!"

Chapter Two

"An excellent idea!" came a wheezy voice from the bathroom, and Edgar Jay, the ghost of an elderly, upright vacuum cleaner trundled out. The bolts on the top of his cloth dustbag shone like two bright eyes gleaming with anticipation, and the long pattern that ran down the bag and looked very like a nose, wrinkled as if sniffing the air.

"It will give me the opportunity to hoover the caravan thoroughly," he huffed happily.

Edgar Jay was proud to be still serving the Ghoulstones – or what was left of them – and was determined to keep up the standards. However, blowing dust about was all the cleaning he'd been able to manage since Flo and Maggot had found him, fifty years before, covered in carrot peelings in a Little Frightley Manor dustbin.

"Don't be a spoilsport, Edgar Jay!" cried Flo. "We're all going to George's school."

"Pirates don't have time for school," said Mary doubtfully.

"Pieces of chalk!" squawked Duck.

"We can't go too far from Little Frightley Manor," said Maggot nervously. "You know what happens to our spectral stuffing."

"Weird and wobbly!" squawked Duck.

Little Frightley Manor and its vast grounds had a spectral pull like a magnet and, if they went too far away, the little spooks began to feel as if someone had pulled their plug out and their spectral stuffing was draining away to nothing. It was this unearthly magnetism that had drawn the ghosts of Mary and Duck back to their old home.

"But don't you remember?" said Flo, her eyes wide with excitement, "George said his school is only round the corner."

"Galleon on port side!" shrieked Duck as a gold car came gliding round from the back of the house. "Captain Flash at the helm!"

Sharren, wearing a gold tracksuit with nail varnish and huge earrings to match, was in the driver's seat.

"Georgie!" she shouted. "Come on!"

"If it isn't far, smarty-phantom," demanded Maggot, poking his snub nose into Flo's face, "why does he go in the car?"

"You know *her*," said Flo scornfully, jerking her thumb at Sharren. "She thinks walking's bad for your health."

The ghosts watched George drag himself over to the car, yank the door open and throw his bags in.

"Come on!" shouted Flo. "It's now or never!"

She bounced out of the caravan and headed for the car, holding up her tattered petticoats. The Ghoulstone ghosts had never mastered the art of floating and tried to run like they had when they were alive. The result was a sort of comical moonwalk.

Maggot wasn't staying at home without his sister.

"Wait for me!" he squealed. He stuffed something squeaky and wriggling under his shirt and chased after Flo.

Mary checked the coast was clear and followed him – she wasn't staying at home without the twins. Duck checked the coast was clear and followed her – he wasn't staying at home without Mary.

As Flo got to the car, she could see George sitting in the back, staring miserably ahead. Sharren started the engine and adjusted the mirror to apply some more gold lipstick. Flo, forgetting she wasn't very good at going through solid objects, leaped head first at the car door. She dived through the closed window as far as her shoulders – and stuck.

"Help me, George!" she laughed, squirming. "I want to come to school with you."

George's face broke into a comical grin. Flo looked like the artificial moose head his father had stuck over the fireplace in the

lounge. He leaned across and pushed the button to open the window. As the window glided down, Flo's head went with it and got embedded in the door.

With a final purse of her gold-coated lips, and a pat of her hair, Sharren released the handbrake. Maggot and Mary quickly scrambled up Flo's back and climbed in through the window.

"I'm not a stepladder," moaned Flo as, with a final heave, she forced her way through the door and into the car. With a flurry of green feathers Duck flew in, and

an excited but nervous pile of ghostly paper settled itself on the parcel shelf.

George looked at his spooky, transparent friends. "This is going to be great!" he exclaimed.

"You've changed your tune, Georgie," remarked Sharren, who had no idea she had so many passengers. "After all that trouble I had getting you out of bed. I'm exhausted from yelling."

Edgar Jay trundled over to wave them off, the crease at the bottom of his bag curling in a happy smile. There was nothing he liked more than the prospect of a good day's cleaning.

"Come with us, Edgar Jay," called Maggot. "It'll be fun."

"Indeed not!" said Edgar Jay, his bag wobbling at the very idea. "Nothing would persuade me to get into that infernal machine. I have never travelled faster than hoovering speed and I do not intend to start now."

But as he turned back to the caravan,

Flo, who wanted everyone to enjoy themselves, suddenly leaned out of the car and dragged him in by the nozzle.

Edgar Jay was horrified. "I say!" he huffed. "Hold fast, Mrs Brussell. I wish to descend from this automobile."

Sharren put her foot down hard. The car sped down the drive, out between the gate-posts with their enormous stone Brussels sprouts, and off to George's school.

Edgar Jay cowered in the corner of the plush leather back seat.

"Slow down, Madam!" he shouted. "Mind that bicycle! Remember the highway code . . ." He covered his mouth with his nozzle. "I think I'm going to be sick!"

"Now, Georgie," Mrs Brussell was saying, "have you got your snack box, book bag, homework diary, football boots . . ."

The ghosts were jostling about excitedly, and Mary, her spyglass to her eye, was keeping lookout through the sunroof.

". . . PE kit, Irish dancing shoes . . ." continued Sharren.

"This is spooktacular!" shouted Flo. "I wish I could have a go at driving."

"You don't know how to drive!" scoffed Maggot.

"I do!"

"You don't!"

"Do!"

"Shut up!" laughed George.

"Georgie!" exclaimed Mrs Brussell, stopping mid-list, braking suddenly with the shock and sending Edgar Jay tumbling on to the floor. "That's no way to speak to your mother."

"Sorry, Mum," smirked George. "I wasn't talking to . . . *Atchoo*! Get your feathers out of my nose, Duck!"

"I'm worried about you, son," sighed Sharren. "You haven't been the same since we came to Little Frightley Manor." She sniffed suspiciously. "Have you been at the bananas?"

They arrived at George's school. Maggot and Flo looked eagerly out of the window.

Mary and Duck peered suspiciously out of the roof. Beyond the school's black railings they could see a long, L-shaped building with huge glass windows. The walls formed two sides of a playground packed full with chattering children.

Maggot pointed to the hopscotch squares. "Someone's painted on the ground!" he said. "They'll be in trouble."

When he was four, Maggot had found a tin of white paint and made a brilliant picture of a hippopotamus on the courtyard in front of Little Frightley Manor. When his mother saw it, she had a fit of the vapours and Maggot didn't get any pudding for three days.

"Ship to port side!" yelled Mary in excitement. "I knows it by its rigging." She pointed at the hall window where the PE ropes were hanging down invitingly.

"Shipshape and seaworthy!" squawked Duck, impressed. "All aboard!"

"Not a boat trip as well!" groaned Edgar Jay, whose bag had turned a faint shade of spectral green.

On the third side of the playground was the crumbling, weather-beaten building which had once been the Little Frightley Village schoolhouse. It stood on its own, a little way from the rest of the school, empty and boarded up for many years. Parked next to it was a van with *Bodgers the Builders – The Best in Bricks, Battlements and Boardings* on the side. The cracked and rotted door of the old building had been forced open, and in front stood the builders, with piles of sand, concrete mixers and cups of tea. The old schoolhouse was about to be turned into a new classroom.

Flo gazed longingly at the roof with its mossy and broken tiles.

"Look at the bell up there!" she sighed. "I bet I could make a lot of noise with that."

George knew that Flo loved fiddling with anything she could get her spectral mitts on, but he didn't think she'd have much luck with the bell. It was old and rusty, and the rope had rotted away years ago.

A note fluttered on to George's lap.

More thoughts about School
by Bartholomew Otherington-Smythe
1. *My spectral stuffing feels strange.*
2. *I recommend returning to Little Frightley*
   Manor.
3. *Sadly.*

"Look at all those children!" said Maggot nervously. "Supposing we're seen by them . . . or the teachers . . . or the builders!"

The little ghosts paled and shrunk back into the leather seats.

"They won't notice you," said George firmly. They were such weedy little spooks that no one ever seemed to see them except for him. "Come into school with me."

But the ghosts had almost vanished into the upholstery.

"Don't be silly, Georgie," said his mother. "Ten-year-old boys can go to school on their own."

As he looked at them, George didn't

think his friends were going to budge, although Edgar Jay was looking longingly at the solid pavement outside.

"Scaredy-ghosts!" he thought to himself. "Oh well, see you tonight, then," he said, bitterly disappointed.

Mrs Brussell gave George a quick air kiss. George dragged himself and his huge bag out of the car and walked as slowly as he could through the school gates. He kept his head down and didn't look back as his mother drove off.

Chapter Three

George walked into his classroom and stopped dead. Something was different, but he couldn't make out what it was at first. The tables were in their usual groups, the walls were still covered in bright pictures, and his classmates were sitting where they always did, chatting and fiddling with their pencil cases.

Then, suddenly, he saw a ghostly vacuum cleaner, pale and wobbly, trundling between the desks, pursued by two singed Victorian spooks. Flo and Maggot were crawling after Edgar Jay on all fours, trying to keep out of sight. Mary was stealthily creeping up on him from behind a bookcase.

"Jumping ship like that," she cursed under her breath. "That ancient dust-blower should be keel-hauled!"

"Wheel-hauled!" squawked Duck, who was stealthily following Mary.

"I apologize for leaving the automobile in such an impolite manner . . ." panted Edgar Jay as he tried to escape them.

"Out the porthole!" shrieked Duck.

". . . but nothing could persuade me to travel with that dreadful driver again."

Edgar Jay had shot out of the window of the Bentley and made for the school as fast as his spectral wheels could carry him, and George had been too sunk in misery to notice the little ghosts dashing past after the hoover.

"You've got to come back with us," whispered Maggot, who was crawling under the desks to head off Edgar Jay.

"The car's long gone, you stupid hoover!" hissed Flo. "Come on, before we're seen!" She looked nervously round the class, and saw George's grinning face at the door.

"I'm so glad you're here," called George, beaming at his ghostly friends. "And look – no one else can see you."

"Sit down please, George," called Mrs Neal, his teacher, feeling resigned. It had been too much to hope that George would have a break from clowning on the first day back.

George sat down next to Tony and watched the little ghosts gradually emerge from their hiding places. Flo sidled up to the overhead projector and looked eagerly at its knobs, and Maggot, still with his wriggling bundle under his shirt, began to inspect the frog's skeleton that Tony had brought in last term. Mary climbed the bookshelves, cutlass between her teeth, with Duck following, pencil in his beak. George could see a pile of paper shrinking on the teacher's desk as Boss helped himself to Mrs Neal's supply.

As soon as Edgar Jay realized he was safe from Mrs Brussell's nightmare taxi-service, he started to hoover the fish tank. George watched the waves and stifled a giggle. He leaned back in his chair towards the projector.

"Are you feeling wobbly at all?" he asked Flo.

"No, George," said Mrs Neal wearily. "But you will if you tip back much further." The class sniggered. They loved it when George started clowning around.

"My fingernails are tingling," said Flo. "But that's all." She twiddled a few knobs. "This is spooktacular!"

"My nose is a bit numb," called Maggot, giving it a test sniff. "But I'm all right."

Mrs Neal called the register.

"How odd," she said as she got to the end. "We seem to have some new children."

The ghosts stared at each other aghast – Mrs Neal *could* see them! The rest of the class looked around for the new faces. Maggot dived under the table, Flo faded with fright, and Mary and Duck prepared to abandon ship.

Mrs Neal read out the names.

1. *Bartholomew Otherington-Smythe.*
2. *Florence Ghoulstone*

George realized that Boss was taking school seriously and he snorted with laughter. The rest of the class joined in as Mrs Neal gave George a suspicious look.

"Another one of your jokes, George?" she said. "Thank you for trying to amuse us but it's time for some work. Now, everyone, I want you to write: 'The best thing about my holiday'."

The little ghosts heaved sighs of relief. They were always scared they would be seen. Not everyone was as sensible as George when it came to spooks, but thankfully very few people ever see ghosts.

"Didn't call *my* name," said a muffled voice from under Maggot's shirt.

Maggot reached inside and gently drew out a long, prickly scroll. It unwound itself to reveal the ghost of an odd-looking hedgehog.

He was as flat as a frisbee, with legs splayed out at the sides, and squashed spines parted in the middle where he'd been sat on by a pot-bellied pig. He came from a family of hedgehogs who still lived under things in the grounds of Little Frightley Manor.

"Never been to school," squeaked the hedgehog, wistfully. His perky, pointed nose sniffed the air. "Call my name. Like a teacher."

"Oh all right!" huffed Flo. "Slightly Flat-Hedgehog?"

"Yes, Miss," squealed Slightly happily. He rolled into George's pencil case and began to snore.

George opened his English book. Mrs Neal would never believe him if he wrote about his ghost friends. He couldn't write about the time Maggot got stuck halfway through the kitchen wall. Or the morning when Mary and Duck boarded the milk float and tried to slit the milkman's throat. He sat and chewed his pen.

"Mrs Neal," called one of the class. "The lights are moving." George waved at Mary who was swinging across the ceiling.

"George, stop flapping and get on with your work," said Mrs Neal crossly. "What's the matter, Amy?"

"Something's blowing round my ankles, Miss."

Edgar Jay was cleaning under the desks.

"It's just a draught, Amy. Close the window please."

"Mrs Neal!" called another voice. "The

frog's legs are jumping!"

The class burst out laughing. This was better than writing.

"Maggot!" giggled George.

"Who are you calling a maggot?" said Tony indignantly.

"George Brussell, leave Tony alone!" said Mrs Neal. "And are you eating? I can smell bananas!" Mrs Neal was beginning to feel irritable. It was only the first day back and already George was winding the class up. "I'm warning you, George. Any more and you'll miss football practice."

This was serious. George thought he'd better get the ghosts to start behaving themselves.

"My pencils keep rolling about, Miss," wailed one of the girls. The phantom parrot was searching a pencil case for hidden treasure.

"Duck!" shouted George.

The class ducked.

"George Brussell!" said his teacher crossly. "Do you have to be the class clown

29

all the time? That's it. No football practice for you today."

George began to wish the ghosts were back at Little Frightley Manor.

"Mrs Neal!" wailed Amy. "Someone's written a list in my book, in fancy handwriting."

"Miss, the projector's going really funny!"

"The frog's still dancing, Miss."

The class were all on their feet, watching the uncanny performance of their possessions and wondering how George was doing it all.

George could feel a total football ban coming on and he couldn't take it any more.

"Why don't you all go home?" he yelled at the ghosts.

Everyone stared at him.

At that moment a bell rang furiously. The deep sound echoed eerily round the class. It made hair stand on end and skin crawl. Mrs Neal shivered and wrapped her cardigan round her.

"It's just the old school bell," she said at last. "The workmen must be doing the roof. Finish your writing, everyone."

The class turned back to their books in silence. George's outburst had been forgotten.

But when the sound of the bell died away, George suddenly noticed the little ghosts standing in a line, pale and still. Then, as if they were summoned in their sleep, they walked like zombies out of the classroom.

31

Chapter Four

The ghosts walked in a silent line down the corridor and out into the playground. George muttered an excuse about the toilet and shot out after them. No one looked up.

"Come back!" he yelled. "I didn't meant to upset you."

But the ghosts didn't turn their heads.

George ran to the front of the line and held his hand out to stop them, but they walked stiffly through him as if he wasn't there. George was taken aback. The ghosts couldn't usually get through solid objects so easily – even Slightly had managed to waddle through his shoe – and they sent a cold tremor through his body.

The ghosts marched slowly and deliberately towards the derelict old schoolhouse. Bodgers were in their van having a well-earned snack, after making one small hole in a wall inside the building.

The ghosts walked past the wheelbarrows and drills and straight in through the open door. George made sure that no one was watching, and followed.

The ghosts stood stock-still in the dark, dusty old schoolroom. The only light came from two tiny windows, and the ghosts' spectral glow was faint in the gloom. They rubbed their eyes as if they had just woken from a heavy sleep and looked around. The room was empty and bare, apart from one wall, which had a very old blackboard nailed on it. There was a hole hacked in the middle of the blackboard, where Bodgers had started work.

"I wish you'd stop mucking about!" complained George, knowing he could be in serious trouble if he was found in the out-of-bounds old schoolhouse. "It isn't funny any more."

But no one was listening.

"How did we get in here?" asked Flo faintly, looking round the cold, bleak room. "I thought we were being called, but there's no one here."

33

"My spectral stuffing feels as if it's falling out," whispered Maggot, pinching himself.

"We've been lured on to the rocks," muttered Mary, searching all the corners for an enemy.

Boss's papers fluttered in a nervous heap on the beam in the roof.

"High and dry!" squawked Duck feebly from a rafter.

"I'm getting awfully short of puff," wheezed Edgar Jay. "I fear we will lose our strength if we do not return to Little Frightley Manor."

"Why don't I see you to the gate?" suggested George quickly. "It won't take you long to get home. You can almost see the house from there."

But before anyone could move, the gloom seemed to stir and, one by one, stretching in orderly rows from the front of the classroom to the back, an army of ghostly desks appeared. In the centre of the room, growing up from the floor, came a spooky old stove and, finally, an eerie teacher's table slowly materialized at the

front of the class. The ghosts shrank and shimmered like flickering candles.

"Wow!" said George, forgetting all about sending his friends home. He pushed his hand through one of the desks. It made his skin tingle. "This is serious spookery. Well done, you Little Terrors! How did you do it?"

But the ghosts were staring at the hole in the blackboard. Something was moving slowly towards them out of the darkness. As it came closer, they could see it was the

figure of a bony old lady carrying a book under her arm.

As soon as the ghosts saw the figure, they knew by her cold, grey glow that she was as dead as they were.

Chapter Five

Miss Charity Lucretia McLeery, once the Little Frightley village schoolmistress, had become a ghost over a hundred years before. One evening, the builders had come to the schoolhouse to put a new blackboard on the wall. The Mr Bodger of that time was in a hurry to get to the pub, and didn't notice he was holding the plans upside-down, so he nailed the new blackboard across the stock cupboard door by mistake. Miss McLeery was in there, busily tidying, and didn't hear the hammering. She continued to reorganize her stock cupboard, pausing only to starve to death and become a ghost, and there she stayed for over a hundred years, until the moment when the builder's pickaxe went through the blackboard.

Miss McLeery had been haunting on her own for so long that she couldn't remember ever being alive. The rude interruption had reminded her that it was time for school, so she had pulled on the phantom rope and rung the bell as usual to summon her pupils for morning lessons.

George watched with interest as the skinny old spook glided towards him.

"I'm George Brussell," he said eagerly, holding out his hand. Chilly atmospheres never put George off and he usually enjoyed meeting new ghosts. "Pleased to meet you."

The ghost ignored him.

"Go to your places," she rasped. Her voice was thin and reedy and seemed to echo round the bare walls of the classroom.

Slightly obeyed immediately by curling up and going to sleep. "Place" to a hedgehog means somewhere to hibernate.

The other little ghosts marched over to the regimented rows of desks that had a slate and chalk waiting on each one. They sat down in the front row, girls on the left and boys on the right. Weakened by being

away from Little Frightley Manor, they found themselves obeying this elderly spirit who had summoned them to her spectral world.

Without thinking, George tried to sit at a ghostly desk at the back and promptly fell through it. He got up and leaned untidily against the wall instead.

"Good morning, school ghouls," said the bony phantom coldly. The little ghosts stared at her. They could see she wore a high-necked blouse and a heavy black skirt that silently swept the floor. They could see her thin face and her grey hair in a bun but everything about her transparent figure was blurred, as if she was standing behind frosted glass.

"Where are your manners?" said the spectre, her voice cracking as if she hadn't used it for a long time. "I have not heard a single 'Good morning, Miss McLeery' from any of you. Is this how you show respect for your teacher?"

George was delighted. He'd never met a

ghost teacher and he wondered why he hadn't seen her at school before. He was willing to bet she couldn't make him do his sums, however hard she tried. Whatever strange influence she had over his friends, it wasn't going to work on him!

"Morning, Miss McLeery," he called cheerfully.

He didn't think he'd show his friends the way home just yet. They were glowing rather faintly, but it wouldn't do the Little Terrors any harm to find out what happened when a teacher could see you and expected you to do as you were told. After all, he was going to miss football because of them.

The old biddy was standing at an empty desk. She picked up a piece of quivering paper and put it as near to her eyes as her long nose would allow. Miss McLeery was short-sighted but she'd put her spectral spectacles down some time in the last hundred years and couldn't remember where. She read aloud:

School – now that I am here
by Bartholomew Otherington-Smythe

1. I like this classroom.
2. The desks are in rows.
3. And so are the pupils.
4. It is quiet.
5. I can concentrate on my lists.
6. I never want to leave.

Miss McLeery glowed briefly with satisfaction. "Not a bad effort from so small a child!" she said to the empty desk. "I see you love your school."

Miss McLeery's past pupils would have been astonished at their teacher's mild behaviour, but the shrivelled old spectre was a bit rusty from her long stay in the stock cupboard. She moved on and stared at Edgar Jay. She didn't remember a one-armed pupil on wheels.

"Are you some factory boy who has met with an unfortunate accident?"

She didn't wait for an answer. Her keen nose had picked up a strange smell of fruit.

47

She peered closely at Maggot and Flo, whose mother obviously didn't change their clothes often enough.

"Disgraceful!" she said. She couldn't recall any of her pupils looking this disreputable.

"We can't help how we look," said Flo. "We got blown up!"

"My pupils do not blow up!" said Miss McLeery, flickering with shock. "Take your slates and write out ten times: 'I must not explode.'"

Flo and Maggot looked at each other. They didn't know how to spell 'explode'.

"We don't do lines at this school," called George. "Why can't they miss their phantom football instead?"

But Miss McLeery was now busy staring at Mary's dirty bare feet, her bloodstained shirt and the dagger sticking out of her chest.

"Disgusting! A girl who fights."

"Course I fights," declared Mary, drawing her cutlass and waving it in the air. "That's what pirates do."

"Stop fidgeting, girl. Learn from the tale of Mad Maud, the girl who brawled."

Miss McLeery opened her favourite book, *Moral Tales for Wicked Children*. She began to read with quiet glee:

"Maud liked nothing more than fighting,
Poking, punching, scratching, biting.
She pinched the footman, pulled his hair.
She pushed poor Nanny down the stairs.

She fought with one, she fought with all.
She fought Big Bert, who was eight feet
  tall.
One day she gave Big Bert a kick.
He beat her brains in with a stick."

She shut the book. A cloud of spectral dust rose from its pages and filled the air. George thought it was a brilliant poem and snorted with laugher.

"Who is that sniggering at the back?" spluttered Miss McLeery, peering through the dusty air.

43

"Don't mind me," called George, waving to her. "I'm only watching."

"*Watching?*" croaked Miss McLeery, taken aback. "Pupils in my class do not watch; they learn. Come here, boy!"

George sauntered down the aisle with his hands in his pockets, whistling tunelessly. He winked at the pale ghosts as he passed. He'd heard that schoolteachers from the old days were really evil, but this one seemed just a doddery old bag. And it would take a lot more spookery than this to bother George.

"You are keen to speak, so answer this," said Miss McLeery. "What is the longest river in Great Britain?"

"You tell me," said George cheekily.

"Insolence!" said Miss McLeery. "It is the Severn."

"I can't think of one," giggled George, "let alone seven!"

The spectre looked at him sternly. "Who won the battle of Stamford Bridge, 1066?" she demanded.

"Probably Chelsea," said George. "Home advantage and all that, but it's a funny time for kick-off."

"You are the most untutored boy I have ever had the misfortune to teach," rasped Miss McLeery, growing angry.

The figure of the hunched old schoolmistress seemed to straighten. It became sharp and clear and glowed harshly in the dull classroom. Now the shivering ghosts could see every pleat of her high-necked blouse, so crisp with starch you could cut your finger on them. Her grey hair

45

was pulled violently back into a tight knot which made her sharp face look even sharper and her pointed nose even longer.

"That's better," said George. "You've come into focus."

Miss McLeery advanced on him, a cold look in her eyes.

"Leave him be, you old shipwreck!" shouted Mary, leaping to her feet.

The old phantom put her sharp nose close to Mary's ear.

"Silence, street urchin!" she hissed.

"Sea urchin!" squawked Duck.

The ghostly teacher froze to the spot. She glared down and saw, for the first time, the one-eyed parrot perched on his desk. She grabbed him round the neck with her skeletal fingers. Duck couldn't move a feather.

"I'm scuppered!" he croaked.

The ghosts trembled as they watched him dangling helplessly like a chicken in a butcher's window. Mary's hand tried to fly to her cutlass, but she found herself sitting

down and feebly reaching for a piece of spectral chalk instead. The longer the ghosts were away from Little Frightley Manor, the weaker they were getting, and they couldn't fight the spectral spell of this spook who was slowly gathering her strength against them. They watched helplessly as Miss McLeery pulled on a rope. A ghostly cage materialized in the air and came down to rest in front of her.

"Don't lock Duck up!" shouted George. "He's a free-range parrot."

"He'll be a stuffed parrot when I've finished with him!" muttered Miss McLeery evilly. She flung Duck into the cage, turning the key that was in the lock, and hoisted it viciously up to the ceiling where it swung from side to side.

"Off to the crow's nest!" squawked the panic-stricken parrot.

George ran over to the nearest window and pulled himself up, using the crumbling brickwork as footholds, until he was sitting on the high window-ledge.

47

Miss McLeery suddenly spotted him.

"Come down, you disobedient school ghoul!" she ordered, her thin lips tightening with anger. "You are not an orang-utan." George was now dangling upside down from a high beam, trying to grab Duck's cage.

"Man the lifeboats!" shrieked Duck, holding on for grim death.

Miss McLeery glided around underneath, waving her book threateningly at George.

"I will not have acrobatic ghouls in my

school," she hissed. "Listen to the tale of Clara Brown, the class clown:

When Clara should have done her sums
She walked the classroom on her thumbs.
When she was told to sit and write
She somersaulted out of sight.

When asked to study from a book
She dangled rudely from a hook.
Each time she got the cane she'd duck it
And one day fell into a bucket."

George realized he couldn't grasp a ghostly cage, so he swung down from his beam and landed on his feet in front of the bony old spook.

"Look, Miss M, I'm not one of your pupils," he said patiently as she stood glaring coldly at him. He flexed his arm proudly. "That's solid muscle, that is, not see-through like you. I'm not a ghost – I'm a living boy!"

"Wash your mouth out with carbolic

soap, you ghastly spook!" Miss McLeery shrieked, shuddering from head to toe. "There's no such thing as the living!" Miss McLeery hadn't breathed for so long that she'd forgotten anybody did. She stared at the class in disgust. "In all my career I have never seen such appalling school ghouls."

"Don't worry about them," said George, soothingly. "You'll never manage to educate that lot. I'll take them home . . ."

But he stopped as he saw the look of stony determination on the old apparition's face.

Miss McLeery's words cut through the air like scissors.

"I will start by giving you all a good thrashing!"

Chapter Six

"There is nothing like the feel of the stick to focus the mind," snarled Miss McLeery. "Stand up and hold your hands out."

The ghost children quivered to their feet and obeyed. Boss's paper rose trembling in the air and Edgar Jay held out his nozzle.

"Come on, you lot," said George. "Eerie old McLeery can't keep you here."

But this was Miss McLeery's spectral world and the little ghosts seemed powerless to escape it.

"Cane!" snapped Miss McLeery.

From the hole in the blackboard appeared a long, glowing stick. The ghost of Miss McLeery's cane, known to her Victorian pupils as Thwacker, wove its way through the air to hover menacingly at her side. A hundred years was a long time for a cane to go without the feel of flesh, living

or otherwise, and Thwacker was hungry for action. He rose up eagerly and made a beeline for Maggot. The singed twin was standing with his hands out ready and his knees knocking – a delightful-looking specimen of spectral jelly. Thwacker was a bully and always went for the easy victim.

But just as the evil cane raised himself over the terrified little ghost's hand, George leaped between them and pulled a face. Thwacker backed off in surprise.

"Call yourself a cane?" mocked George. "I've seen better sticks propping up the runner beans."

"Thrash him!" shrieked Miss McLeery. Her shrill voice echoed round the rafters.

George stepped up to Thwacker. Flo gasped and Maggot covered his eyes.

"Go on then," taunted George. "Dare you!"

George wasn't sure what a ghost could do to living flesh, but he was certain it would do a lot of damage to his friends' spectral stuffing.

Thwacker slashed at him, passed straight through and clattered to the floor. He picked himself up crossly, wondering how he'd failed to hit such a solid target. He whacked at George's back, at his legs, at his arms, but George just laughed – it felt like pins and needles. Thwacker thought he must be losing his touch – for the first time in his illustrious career as a champion whacker he had not reduced his victim to a sobbing heap. He turned his attention to more likely subjects, and made for Flo, who cowered behind her desk as he approached.

"Over here, Sticky!" jeered George. "I've seen more frightening sticks in a box of matches."

This was too much for a cane with a reputation to defend. Thwacker turned from Flo and chased after George, cutting and slashing. George dodged round the stove, and then, to Miss McLeery's astonishment, ploughed straight through a whole line of desks as if they weren't there. It felt like running through bubble bath.

"Unruly ghoul!" shrieked the furious phantom. "Have you no respect for the furniture?"

"Funny thing," said George, stopping suddenly. "My mum's always saying that."

Thwacker skidded to a halt in mid-air and, before he knew what was happening, Miss McLeery had knocked him aside.

"Useless piece of wood!" she barked. "I will do the job myself."

Thwacker mooched over to the corner for a good sulk. He was a fine young stick, without a trace of woodworm, and his talents were being wasted. He hadn't had such a bad day since old McLeery had wielded him at Charlotte Bodger, missed and concussed him on the desk instead. If she couldn't find him a victim who would keep still then she should be pensioned off.

Meanwhile Miss McLeery began rolling up her sleeves, slowly and venomously.

"I will brook no disobedience in my class," she hissed at the petrified little ghosts, and turned to deal with her unruly pupil. But as soon as Miss McLeery had dismissed the cane, George knew this was his chance to save his friends. He would act as a decoy.

"You lot go home!" he yelled, dashing to the door, where he put his fingers in his mouth and whistled loudly at the old spook. Miss McLeery spun round to see him running across the netball court, jumping and waving his arms at her. She strode purposefully after him, her book of moral tales under her arm.

But when she reached the door, she stopped. This was the boundary of her classroom, the edge of her spectral world. It was as if cling film was stretched across the opening. Miss McLeery had died long before cling film was invented, but nevertheless, she could feel an invisible, sticky barrier stopping her getting at her wayward pupil. Her bony fingers scrabbled in vain as if she was caught in a gigantic spider's web. And, at that moment, her long, pointed nose came into its own. As she poked it forward to keep sight of her prey, its sharp end

pierced the invisible force field and, with an eerie pop, she was out.

The minute Miss McLeery's nose broke the spectral barrier, her strange, ghostly aura began to leak out from the old schoolroom. Miss McLeery belonged in the Victorian classroom, but once she had left it, she somehow had the power to start dragging time back to her own era. This worked easily against the feeble ghosts trapped in the old schoolhouse, but in the unknown, modern world of George's school it was a different matter. Miss McLeery's power was a bit rusty after so many years in a

cupboard, so it began to come out in dollops like tomato ketchup from a bottle, popping up here and there.

Mrs Neal's class went back two hours, completely forgot that George had been in that morning, and started the school day again. The head teacher unexpectedly put her coat on and went home for yesterday's tea. A group of infants, who'd been in the middle of PE in the hall, suddenly poured out into the playground in their shorts for last year's sports day.

Miss McLeery stopped aghast at the sight of all the bare knees running amok around her. Why were these unruly ghouls not in school?

"You will remember Beatrice Brass, the truant from class," she yelled, shaking her book at them:

"*She ran from her teacher and out of school,
And was trampled to bits by a passing mule.*"

The children in the playground couldn't see the old phantom but, as Miss McLeery glided towards them, they could feel her ghostly teacher's power.

"Stand in line!" she snapped. "Punishment – physical exercises. One, two, one, two!"

The infants stopped playing, formed straight lines and began, in a sort of trance, to swing their arms and march on the spot.

Miss McLeery suddenly spied George, who was waving at her from halfway up a netball post, and strode towards him, calling over her shoulder, "Tell your mothers that in future they must not send you to school in your undergarments!"

As she chased George into the school, the children gradually stopped their exercises and wondered why on earth they were outside without any plimsolls on.

In the school hall there was a class of children queuing at the dinner hatch for a lunch they'd had three weeks ago – and it was only half past ten.

"Right, ladies, scrap the roast dinner," Mrs Craddock, the chief cook, was hurriedly telling her staff. "The clock must have stopped. It'll have to be a quick sausage and chips – or salad – or something!"

George burst into the hall and thought of hiding behind the bookshelves in the library corner, but two children were already there, working on the computer. He ran on past the line of pupils, who were chattering excitedly as they began to smell their favourite meal being cooked. Miss McLeery followed him through the swing doors of the hall, and the children stood to attention as she passed. Unseen by the busy dinner ladies, George crept into the kitchen and dived into a food cupboard. Miss McLeery followed and peered shortsightedly round the kitchen for him.

She sniffed the air. "Just as I thought!" she muttered, forgetting about George for the moment. "These children are being overfed. There is nothing like hunger to focus the mind. School ghouls just need a little school gruel, or they will be like Billy Button, the class glutton:

> *Billy liked to eat and eat.*
> *It caused his brain to overheat.*
> *And so the child was quite unable*
> *To learn his twenty-three times table."*

From his cupboard George could hear Miss McLeery muttering to herself. When he poked his head out, his nostrils were hit by the most disgusting stink he had ever smelt in his life. The dinner ladies had fallen under Miss McLeery's spectral spell and, like a blank-faced line of robots, were working over pans which bubbled and boiled with an utterly nauseous odour. The old ghost may not have believed in the living, but she believed absolutely in a daily dose of school gruel.

The sausage and chips were left forgotten in the ovens. As George watched, the army of dinner ladies heaved the heavy pot over to the serving hatch and dolloped a spoonful of gruel on to each plate as the children went past. George was knocked back into the cupboard by the smell.

Although the children in the hall weren't near enough to be mesmerized by the ghost, they were certainly affected by the gruel.

"This is disgusting!" one child called.

"It's worse than my dad's cooking!" groaned another.

"I think I'm going to be sick!"

Now that the eerie old ghoul had found other pupils to discipline, her power began to leave the old schoolroom. George's friends started to feel stronger. Timidly, they left their desks.

"Do you think she's caught George?" quavered Flo.

"She'll be coming back for us," wailed Maggot, shimmering weakly.

A hurried list appeared on the broken blackboard.

Things to do
by Bartholomew Otherington-Smythe
1. *Vacate this classroom immediately.*
2. *Return to Little Frightley Manor.*
3. *Do not delay.*

"But Boss," gasped Flo. "We can't leave George!"

"Let's join battle!" yelled Mary.

"Don't forget your shipmate, shipmates!" squawked Duck, rattling his cage.

Flo and Mary pulled on the rope, the cage crashed on to a desk and Maggot turned the key in the lock. Duck fell out on his back.

"Rough seas!" he squawked feebly.

"My dear young Ghoulstones," puffed Edgar Jay, "we must find Master George."

"Come on, Slightly!" called Maggot to the snoring hedgehog.

The ghosts turned to the door. But there was Thwacker, weaving evilly in front of them like a deadly cobra. Although he was fed up with his mistress, he was a loyal old

stick at heart, and here, at last, was a chance to punish her school ghouls.

Thwacker set about his task with glee.

Chapter seven

Thwacker hadn't had such a good day since Miss McLeery had lined up seventy-three snivelling Victorian schoolchildren for six of the best. Four hundred and thirty-eight thwacks in one session, and now he was well on the way to beating that record. He wasn't going to let any of the little ghosts escape – not even the invisible one with the paper.

Flo and Maggot dived under desks and cowered in corners but couldn't avoid the stinging lashes. Thwacker interrupted Slightly's hibernation and gave the little hedgehog a terrible headache and some more broken prickles. Edgar Jay tried to defend himself with his nozzle, but it was hard to see in the weird snowstorm of Duck's feathers and Boss's lists, and the cane knocked all the puff out of his bag.

Thwacker's victims were beginning to ooze blue spectral stuffing. Only Mary had dodged the cane's vicious attack. But now he floated silently up behind the pirate and slashed at her head. However, six years rampaging round the Spanish Main had made Mary a most skilful nine-year-old swordsgirl, and before Thwacker could defend himself, she spun round, her cutlass moving like lightning through the air. In a second, Thwacker lay in seven bits on the floor.

"Pieces of eight!" she yelled triumphantly.

Her day in school hadn't taught Mary how to count.

"Make haste, everyone," wheezed Edgar Jay weakly.

The ghosts made for the door, clutching their wounds, but as they came to the pile of sticks, the pieces of cane began to twitch. Seven little Thwackers rose up and advanced in a grim line towards the quavering ghosts, who backed away.

Suddenly an inky piece of paper appeared in the air. A pair of invisible hands screwed it up into a ball and threw it feebly at the little sticks.

"Good idea, Master Bartholomew," puffed Edgar Jay. "But you are in need of extra impetus. Allow me to assist."

As Boss screwed up the paper, Edgar Jay huffed and puffed and blew with the little strength he had left. The inky balls were fired at the Thwackers like cannonballs.

"Direct hit amidships!" squawked Duck.

"Down like ninepins!" shouted Mary.

The mini Thwackers picked themselves up and flew through the air in a furious squadron. They began to tap and prod at the little ghosts' eyes and ears, and poke up their noses, like a swarm of very angry wasps. The ghosts fell to their knees – all except Edgar Jay who didn't have any. But then Duck suddenly came to the rescue. With a flurry of green feathers, he swooped down and gathered up the pieces of Thwacker in his beak.

"Gox 'em up!" he muttered out of the corner of his mouth.

"What's he saying?" asked Maggot.

Duck jumped up and down frantically on Miss McLeery's table, flapping his wings.

"Gox ''em up!"

The little Thwackers were jostling in his beak, threatening to escape.

"Gox 'em up – in a gesk!"

"Box them up in a desk!" yelled Flo. "Great idea, Duck."

The ghosts struggled to raise the desk lid with the cage on top. Duck spat the seven little canes inside the desk and they slammed the lid shut. Angry tapping noises were heard as the sticks jumped up and down.

"Pipe down there below deck!" called Mary. "Or we'll have 'ee for firewood!"

There was immediate silence in the desk. The ghosts raised a feeble cheer.

"Seven bits of stick in a dead man's desk!" crowed Duck. "Yo ho ho and a bottle of ink!"

"Let's find George," said Maggot weakly.

*

George slipped out from his hiding place in the food cupboard and looked around the kitchen. Mrs Craddock was sobbing in a corner and being comforted by her staff. She'd been school cook of the year three years running, and nothing like this had ever happened to her before. She'd had to throw away a hundred and fifty burnt sausages and thirty bags of oven chips, and had no idea why she'd thought the children would prefer the disgusting slop that was stinking out her kitchen.

George crept out into the hall and crouched down behind the piano. He could see plates of uneaten gruel, a class of green-faced children sitting at the dinner tables, and the pale, glowing figure of Miss McLeery peering through a classroom door that led off from the hall. She must still be looking for him.

Some of the children in the classroom were cheerfully constructing a model of the Tower of London from cereal boxes, and another group was painting a figure of

68

Anne Boleyn. They were covered in red paint. This was one classroom that the old spook's spectral power hadn't reached – yet.

Miss McLeery's face was open-mouthed with horror. Everywhere she looked there were school ghouls chattering, school ghouls milling about, school ghouls messing about with paint. The desks were not in rows, there was no punishment cage, and no one was being whacked. And worse than all this – the pupils seemed to be enjoying school!

"I must put a stop to this outrage! I will work on these ignorant and wayward ghouls. I will fill every head with rules and every belly with gruel, and in the end their own mothers won't recognize them!"

She walked over to the serving hatch and grasped the handle of the dinner bell in her bony fingers. As she gathered all her spectral strength, the bell began to ring, louder and louder, summoning every living child in Little Frightley School.

Chapter Eight

The children of Little Frightley Village School filed into the hall at the sound of the dinner bell, which was guaranteed to summon everyone for one of Mrs Craddock's lunches. The children whispered and nudged each other.

"What's that dreadful smell?"

"Where's my dinner?"

"I feel sick!"

George was relieved. The children obviously couldn't see the old bag and would soon get fed up and go back to their classes.

However, something was happening to Miss McLeery. She seemed to be growing taller and more commanding by the second. George realized she was hovering above the ground. He was impressed – his little friends couldn't raise themselves more than ten centimetres off the floor, and that usually ended in disaster.

The bright hall, with its colourful wall paintings, was becoming dull and gloomy, like an old brown and white photograph. It was as if the evil spectre was sucking the colour from everything to turn Little Frightley Village School into a sepia copy of her drab Victorian classroom. The hall was lit only by her cold, grey glow. The chattering died away.

Miss McLeery floated in front of the now silent school. She looked icily at the children, some in their PE kit, some covered in paint and some still green from lunch, and one or two very large ones at the back – the teachers had obeyed the summons as well.

"Sort out these desks!" she commanded.

There was no trace now of the croaky old schoolmistress who had first appeared from behind the broken blackboard. Miss McLeery's voice was as sharp as a butcher's knife. It cut through the air, and somehow,

although the old phantom couldn't be seen or heard, her words penetrated into the brains of her new pupils. There was not a sound as the children obediently lifted the tables and chairs and placed them in long rows from the front to the back of the hall.

"Sit down, everyone," said the phantom in a voice like barbed wire. They all obeyed the command – even the teachers. The girls sat on the left and the boys on the right.

George couldn't believe they were doing

what this spectral old bag was telling them – after all, he could see her and he wasn't obeying. But then George Brussell was a very straightforward boy who generally took ghosts in his stride. And anyway, he always had trouble doing as he was told.

Miss McLeery floated up and down the lines of motionless pupils, and finally came to rest in front of the school.

"Now your education can begin in earnest." For the first time, she smiled. It was a terrible, toothless smile. "But we have so much time to make up for, and I must set about correcting the abominable behaviour I have witnessed here. So, you will all be staying behind after school – *for ever!*"

George had a sick feeling in the pit of his stomach, as if he'd had a bowl of ghostly gruel. He didn't fancy the idea of spending the rest of his life cooped up in a Victorian classroom with this horrible harridan – especially if it meant gruel on the menu. He leaped out from behind the piano.

73

"Get out, everyone!" yelled George. "You've got to escape."

Miss McLeery spun round.

"Ah, the ignorant boy who believes in the living," she snarled, remembering what trouble George had caused. "I will make an example of you. And you will thank me. You do not want to be like Arthur Fuddy, who would not study:

As he had never learnt to read,
A vital sign he could not heed,
In letters bold: 'Beware thin ice'.
Young Arthur vanished in a trice."

Eerie McLeery loomed over George, and he recoiled at the sight of her face. Her skin was now stretched tight over her spectral skull. Her grey hair sprang out of its bun and snaked wildly round her head. Her eyes glowed vividly, and George recognized the one weapon against which he had no defence – the Teacher's Glare. All teachers have a look; they learn it at college. Mrs

74

Neal's glare could stop a child at ten paces, the Head's could reduce you to a quivering jelly. But Miss McLeery's burning glare was like nothing he had ever seen, and it pinned George to the spot.

"You are a disgrace to my school!" she spat. "I will cram your empty head so full of knowledge your skull will burst. Then you'll be sorry that you ever dared to misbehave."

"I'll report you," shouted George desperately. "I'll tell Ofsped inspectors about you."

75

George knew he was clutching at straws, but surely there must be an Office of Spectral Education or something that could sort her out.

Miss McLeery began to recite. She rapped out the monarchs of England since Edward the Confessor, the counties and their acreage, the flora and fauna of the British countryside, the Greek alphabet and the Corn Laws.

George tried not to listen to the relentless voice, but he could feel his head buzzing. By the time the awful apparition got to the annual rainfall in the Amazon Basin, everything George knew about calculators, computers and comics had been pushed out of his brain. He couldn't remember when he was born, where he lived, or, more importantly, who was top of the Premiership. His head was full of dry and dusty Victorian facts. His brain was swelling. It would burst through his skull. His head would explode and bits of grey matter would be splattered all over the

piano. George normally enjoyed a bit of gore, but this was too much, even for him – especially as it would be *his* gore. He slumped to his knees, clutching his head to hold it together.

At that moment the battered band of little ghosts limped into the hall, searching for George and nursing their wounds, which still oozed spectral stuffing. They took one look at Miss McLeery hovering over her victim and knew George was in deadly trouble – and that they were his only chance of escape. There was no time to lose. Any minute now she might turn and freeze them to the spot. Flo and Maggot crept up behind the ghost teacher while Mary and Duck shinned up the wall-bars ready to attack. The old spectre, her eyes boring into her helpless victim, was listing with evil relish the symptoms of the Bubonic Plague.

"Get up, George," whispered Maggot urgently. George lifted his heavy head and stared at him blankly. "It's me, Maggot. You know . . . Magnus."

"Magna Carta," chanted George. "Runnymede Green – Anno Domini 1215."

"You must flee," warned Mary.

"Flea," said George, like an automaton. "Noun. Wingless, agile, blood-sucking insect . . ." His eyes cleared for a second and a flash of recognition passed over his bloodless face. "Help me!" he appealed to the ghosts. "I'm a victim of Victorian Education."

Behind him, the whole school was beginning to chant. They started in a whisper:

"Once seventeen is seventeen, twice seventeen is thirty-four, thrice seventeen is fifty-one . . ."

Gradually, the chanting became louder and louder. And above the nightmare of the seventeen times table, the ghastly ghost was screaming at George. Her face was now little more than a skeleton. Her eyes were burning with hatred and her long, pointed nose seemed to stab at him with every word. George felt as if his skull was going to crack. He collapsed under the piano.

Chapter Nine

Without a thought for their own safety, the Little Terrors leapt into action.

"Scuttle the old hulk!" squawked Duck.

"Spike her!" came a little voice from under Maggot's shirt.

Maggot and Flo tried to stamp on Miss McLeery's boots until they realized her feet were nowhere near the floor. Edgar Jay wheeled back to take a determined trundle at her, and Boss prepared a fleet of paper aeroplanes, just like George had taught him in the holidays. But Miss McLeery was now so demented with anger that she was directing all her eerie energy at George, the worst school ghoul she had ever come across. She barely noticed the little figures – until Mary, with a blood-curdling yell, swung past her nose on a PE rope, to land lightly on the computer table in the library

corner. She drew her cutlass and swished it menacingly in the air.

"Fill heads with knowledge, would you?" she shouted. "I'll fill yours with cold steel!"

Duck flapped round and round the spectre's head.

"Skewer her skull! The cross old bones!" he squawked.

Miss McLeery turned her teacher's glare on Mary and stepped towards her. At that moment, Edgar Jay trundled up at top hoovering speed, nozzle at the ready, to knock her over. He missed completely, shot past and got his nozzle embedded in a bookcase.

"I fear I miscalculated my run-up," he wheezed, trying to pull himself out of the sports section of the library.

Mary, transfixed by the ghostly teacher's glare, was standing like a statue on the computer. Miss McLeery advanced on her.

"You guttersnipe! Come down immediately from this . . ." She stopped. Her gaze

had fallen on to the computer. The whole screen was covered in complicated multiplication. Her eyes lit up and she gradually sank until her feet touched the floor. ". . . from this machine!" she murmured.

She swept Mary off the table, put her pointed nose up to the screen and checked the answers.

"All correct!" she said in surprise. "What a wonderful piece of apparatus – but how does it work?"

Forgetting everything else, Miss McLeery began to examine the computer and its keyboard. Gradually, as she concentrated all her spectral energy on this novel machine, the children of Little Frightley Village School emerged from their stupor. They stretched and yawned.

"What are we doing in here?"

"Where's my dinner?"

"I still feel sick."

The teachers, looking very lost, led their classes back to their rooms. No one saw George under the piano.

George lifted his head and opened his heavy eyes. He had the worst headache of his life but he could remember his address, his birthday and every team in the football league. He crawled out from under the piano and staggered towards the little ghosts.

"Boy!" screeched the spectre. "Come here!"

George had no strength to disobey. Miss McLeery's bony finger was stabbing accusingly at the computer screen.

"Explain this device!" she barked. "I cannot get it to obey."

George's jaw dropped open. One minute she had been out to destroy him, and now she wanted him to teach her computing. He had to be careful – this could be a trick.

"It's a computer," he said cautiously. "There's a mouse for . . ."

"Kill it at once!" shrieked Miss McLeery, leaping on to a chair.

"This is the mouse," said George, patiently, picking it up. "It won't run up your skirt . . . if you're nice to it. Look, you use it to control that arrow there." He pointed to the screen. "Then you'll be in charge."

George watched her climb down.

"Hmm . . ." she snorted with a shiver. "Seems like a well-behaved rodent, although it does have rather a long tail."

She began to fiddle gingerly with the mouse.

George felt it was only a matter of time before she lost interest. He could take his friends home now, but what about tomorrow? Would she be waiting to continue his fatal education? His brain felt as heavy as a Christmas pudding.

But then, as if he had found the lucky charm in the middle, the answer came to him.

"Have a go at this, Miss McLeery," he suggested. He clicked on an icon at the bottom of the screen and up flashed:

Spooky School
Solve the sums before the ghost teacher gets you.

"The instructions are on the screen," he said. "You have to escape from the school before the ghost teacher captures you."

Miss McLeery looked at the frightful figure on the screen, running up and down waving its cane. She grabbed the mouse firmly and tried to bash the figure with it. Before she had a chance to crack the screen, George intervened.

"Miss McLeery," he said firmly. "You'll

84

upset the mouse. Try this instead." He
showed the puzzled old ghost how to
complete each sum that appeared on the
screen.

"It's my turn now!" she snapped.

George backed away and watched the
skinny spectre jumping up and down in her
seat as she battled against the computer.
After a moment, he decided to see if it was
safe to go.

"Miss McLeery?" he called.

There was no answer, just a furious
clicking as Miss McLeery's game sprite was
pursued round the graphic corridors.

"Miss McLeery!" he yelled.

"Not now, boy!" She dismissed him with a wave of her skinny arm. "I'm on level thirteen and she has me trapped in the boys' toilets. Now if I can just do this bit of algebra before she reaches the sinks . . ."

George felt it was safe to go. He knew only too well what happened to adults once they got on a computer. It was lucky that the Friends of Little Frightley Village School had just raised enough money to replace this particular one with a brand-new model. The Safe-in-our-Hands Security Company were going to buy the old one. Little did the buyers know, thought George, that they would be getting an extra pair of hands to help their nightwatchman – someone who would soon be teaching burglars a thing or two.

Chapter Ten

Maggot and Duck circled round Miss McLeery, keeping guard on her, while Flo and Maggot grabbed hold of Edgar Jay's bag and pulled him free from the bookcase. George saw sheets of ghostly paper making themselves into a pile in the middle of the hall.

"What do you think of school now, Boss?" he asked. A list was put in front of him.

Education
by Bartholomew Otherington-Smythe

1. Children should be given their daily gruel.
2. Children should be given a daily thrashing.
3. Children should be seen and not heard.
4. Or in my case, not seen and not heard.

"I fear the unspeakable spectre still has

one student," puffed Edgar Jay, straightening his squashed nozzle. "We must take him back to Little Frightley Manor immediately."

The list was snatched from the air and another put hastily in its place.

Apologies, etc.

1. *Sorry – wrong list.*
2. *And please forgive my hurried handwriting.*
3. *In this list, I mean.*
4. *I am in a rush to correct any false impression that I might have given.*
5. *I am sorry if I gave you to believe that I am in favour of gruel.*
6. *Or thrashing.*
7. *I apologize for wishing to come to school.*
8. *End of apologies.*
9. *I apologize for such a long list.*

"Let's go home," said Flo weakly. She looked pale and was barely shimmering.

"Prickles have lost their point," squeaked Slightly from inside Maggot's grimy shirt.

"Come on," said George, "I'll take you to the gate."

The ghosts trailed along behind him and out into the playground. George's head still hurt a bit, but he felt his brain was back to its normal bubbly self. He was slightly worried that he could still list every Corn Law from 1360 to 1846, but that might come in useful if he ever got into conversation with a farmer.

The playground was full of children with their coats and bags, heading for the gates. George saw Tony.

"What's going on?" George asked, puzzled.

"I thought you weren't in today," said Tony in surprise. "Anyway, we're all going home. There's an outbreak of food poisoning – isn't it great!"

"That'll be the gruel," thought George.

He could see his mother's gold car at the gates. Although Mrs Neal and her class had completely forgotten about George, his name had been ticked in the register so

the secretary had phoned Sharren. The poor secretary was still in her office, trying to find phone numbers for the new children at the end of Mrs Neal's register and wishing she knew where the Head had gone.

The little ghosts ran for the car with Edgar Jay trundling at the front.

"Home, madam," he yelled as he tumbled in through the open window, "and don't spare the horses."

Flo and Maggot jostled for the seat next to Sharren.

"I'm going in the front," said Maggot, "with Slightly."

"You're not!" said Flo, trying to elbow him out of the window.

"I am!" shouted Maggot, as he pushed Flo into the glovebox.

"Not!" came Flo's muffled voice.

Sharren, who was filing her nails while she waited for George, sniffed and started hunting round for the banana skin that he must have dropped earlier.

George couldn't go home without one last

look at the old schoolhouse. He sidled up
to the door, trying to look inconspicuous,
not knowing what he would find. He
slipped in and saw the room was completely
empty. There were no desks, no slates, no
sign of a cage – and no builders. They were
probably having lunch at the pub across the
road.

George crept over and poked his head
through the hole in the blackboard. At first
he couldn't see anything in the gloom, but
as his eyes got used to the dark, he made

out the shape of a long thin stick propped in a corner, and he spotted a mouldering old book open on the floor. Somehow he was sure that if he looked any further he would see, slumped in a corner, the grinning skeleton of an old Victorian schoolmistress.